Published by KHARIS PUBLISHING, imprint of KHARIS MEDIA LLC.

All KHARIS PUBLISHING products are available at special quantity discounts for bulk purchases for sales promotions, premiums, fund-raising, and educational needs.

For details, contact:

Kharis Media LLC

Tel: 1-630-909-3405

support@kharispublishing.com

www.kharispublishing.com

Praises for
Shine Your Light

When God blessed us with our son through adoption, I swore that was the most important thing I would teach him; God's Word, how to spot Jesus in every circumstance, and to allow himself to be moved to action by belief.

"Shine Your Light" hit all those points! I'm weeping, because so many mamas will read this book, and build up a Godly generation, for a thousand generations!
I pray it hits them as hard as it hits me. It all starts in the car! At the breakfast table. Finding shoes and homework. The night before. In the womb.

In the private recesses of our hearts, minds, homes and lives. To walk out of belief, in such a way that it comes back around and around, and you and your generations after, can see and say, every day, Jesus for the Win!!!
—**Juli Tapken,** award-winning actress "Providence" and recording artist

***

"Remember, He is with you, right here in your heart. Shine your light, sharing the love of Jesus is the perfect start. He will guide you."

This is how God wants us to live our lives. To love one another as HE has loved us.
We are all God's children, so how perfectly fitting for Courtney to incorporate it into a Childrens Book.

It reminds me of paying it forward. You don't realize how a small act of kindness can affect someone and ultimately change the world one person at a time.

Courtney uses Gods number one commandment to touch children in a way that they will be able to understand. It shows that one person /child can make a huge difference when they shine the light of Jesus. I love how it completes the circle and reaches Shaun in the end even though that was not the intention of Shaun.
Even though this is a children's book, we as adults can also learn from this and shine our light to make the world a better place.
—**Travis Hancock,** award-winning actor- "A Father's Fight"

***

Train up a child in the way they should go is the moral of "Shine Your Light" ...and its payoff, is a legacy of changed lives that will never be the same.

—**Cameron Arnett,** award-winning actor- "Don't Say My Name" "Trafficked",
Producer, and Director

***

"Shine Your Light" repeats throughout the book memorable experiences children experience in school. This children's storybook captures great examples for a caregiver to teach how to Shine your light and love for Jesus.

—**Jenn Gotzon,** award-winning actress-producer "The Farmer and The Belle"

***

"Shine Your Light" is a very inspirational book. It shows how a student uses Jesus to help guide him as he attends a new school. This story is a great example of how we should be using Jesus to guide us every day. Also, just a small gesture that we give someone may be what they need to turn their bad day into a good day. This book is a must read to show how our light for Jesus can shine and how to be a light for others.

—**Rose Taylor,** Reading Recovery Teacher and Interventionist

***

Shine Your Light is a beautiful children's story authored by Miss Courtney Lee Simpson. In an age where our children are constantly bombarded by negativity and questionable behaviors on television and through various social media outlets, the book demonstrates a refreshing approach on to how we as humans can alter the existence of others in a positive manner. By practicing the wisdom of the Golden Rule and the beneficial teachings of Christianity and faith, a divine message is networked to those directly affected and then consistently shared to others in a similar form. Miss Simpson uses examples that most children will experience at some point in their everyday lives, but then illustrates how the multiple acts of kindness can spread to so many others. Also refreshing is the message to children is that is OK to act differently compared to others, and spread kindness to our most vulnerable fellow human beings.

—**William E. Harris,** Cardiovascular Perfusion Specialist, Public Speaker, and Actor

Courtney Lee Simpson

Shine Your Light

Illustrated by
Luigi A. Cannavicci

Shaun sat in the passenger seat of his mom's car. He was extremely nervous about starting at a new school. He said,

"I don't want to go in; I do not want to go to school."

"Shaun, I know a new school can be a scary place," his mom said.

"You need to walk through those doors with a smile on your face..." Shaun interrupted,

"But Mom, I don't know anyone. People may not like me. How do I talk to kids I don't know?"

Shaun's mom continued,
    "Remember, HE is with you, right here in your heart.
    Shine your light. Sharing the love of Jesus is the
    perfect start. HE will guide you."

All of a sudden, Shaun wasn't nervous anymore. He smiled at his mom as she stopped at the drop off area, then jumped out of the car, walked to the school door, took a deep breath and opened it.

Shaun saw a girl who fought back tears as she looked at her books scattered on the floor. He walked over and bent down to help her pick them up. Shaun said,

"I am sorry you're sad. Let me help you."

The girl could not believe someone was helping her. Kids usually knocked the books out of her hands. She said,

"Thank you! My name is Sara. What's your name?"

"You're welcome, Sara. My name is Shaun."

Sara continued,
   "You don't know how much I appreciate your help.
   What can I do for you?"
   "Remember, HE is with you, right here in your heart,"
Shaun told Sara.
   "Shine your light. Sharing the love of Jesus is
      the perfect start. HE will guide you."

Sara said,
    "I will. Thanks again, Shaun."
Shaun walked away.

Sara took her books and walked down the hall. She saw a boy named David stumble and fall to the floor with a loud thud. She ran to help him. She put down her books and reached out her hand to pull him up.

David smiled and said,
   "Thank you. I can be so
   clumsy. I'm late for
   class, but is there
   anything I can do
   for you?"
Smiling back, Sara said,
   "Remember, David, HE is
   with you, right here
   in your heart.
   Shine your light.
   Sharing the love
   of Jesus is the
   perfect start.
   HE will guide you."
David looked at Sara
and said,
   "I will."

Later that day, looking for a chance
to share what he'd heard,
David noticed that Mary forgot her lunch.

He walked over and sat beside her. He asked,
"Didn't you bring a lunch?"
"No," Mary said. "I forgot my lunch.
I don't have money to get anything, either."

David reached in his pocket, but he didn't have any money. He said,
    "Here, you can have half my lunch and more if you need it.
     I have plenty."
Mary's smile was so big and bright it could have lit up the room.
She said,
    "You have no idea how much I appreciate this."
    "You can repay me by shining your light," David said.
    "Shining my light?" asked Mary.
He continued,
    "Share Jesus. Remember, HE is with you, right here in your heart.
     Sharing the love of Jesus is the perfect start."
Mary said,
    "You know what? I will. Thanks, David."

Outside at recess, Mary spotted Leah,
who never had anyone to talk to or play with,
and decided she was going to talk with Leah.
   "Leah will you play with me?" Mary asked.
   "The swings are open."
                      Leah grinned,
                         "Yea, sure.
                            Thanks for being a friend."

They ran to the open swings and tried to see
who could go higher. When the bell rang to
come back indoors, Leah said,

"Mary, how can I ever thank you for
playing with me?"

Mary said,

"Remember, HE is with you, right here in
your heart. Shine your light. Sharing
the love of Jesus is the perfect start.
HE will guide you."

Smiling and hugging Mary, Leah said,

"I will."

When Leah returned to class, she saw Peter digging in his pocket to give Mr. Key money for a snack but overheard him tell Mr. Key he didn't have any money. Leah reached in her pocket and said,

"Don't worry, Peter, I have money you can have."
Mr. Key and Peter both smiled.

Mr. Key exclaimed,
"That was very nice
of you Leah!"
"Yes, it was!
Thank you so much," said Peter.
"You're welcome," Leah said.
Peter said,
"I'll pay you back."

Leah said,
    "No need, Peter. You can repay me by sharing Jesus.
    Remember, HE is with you, right here in your heart. Shine your light.
    Sharing the love of Jesus is the perfect start. HE will guide you."

On the bus, Peter noticed a new kid who didn't have a seat and he offered,

"Hey, you can sit with me."

Shaun, the new kid, sat down next to Peter. Shaun said,

"Thank you, my name is Shaun."

"My name's Peter. You're in my class, aren't you?"

"I think so," Shaun said, recognizing Peter. "I'm trying to meet people and make friends. It is tough being new."

"Well, we can be friends, and tomorrow I'll introduce you to a few of my other friends. We can all hang out," said Peter.

Filled with joy, Shaun said,

"Thank you so much. I really appreciate it. What can I do for you?"

Peter said,
   "Just remember,
   HE is with you, right here in
   your heart. Shine your light.
   Sharing the love of
   Jesus is the perfect
   start. HE will
   guide you."

With a gigantic grin on his face, Shaun
thought to himself, Jesus for the win!

Just after the bus rolled out of sight, Mr. Key arrived home and walked inside. His pregnant wife was sitting on the couch reading a book. With a smile on his face, Mr. Key said,

"I heard something today that I just can't get out of my head. You know, you think you are the teacher, but then along comes a kid who teaches you something. I have no idea how it started, but I know I was supposed to hear it."

"Come and sit with me," said his wife.

Mr. Key sat down on the couch next to his
wife and she asked,
     "What is it, sweetheart?"
     "One of my students reminded me of the
       importance of sharing Jesus. Now,
       I want to share Jesus with everyone,
       especially you and our unborn daughter,"
       said Mr. Key.

He kissed her cheek and placed
his hand on his wife's belly . He whispered,
     "I can't wait to meet you, Kelly. Always remember,
       HE is with you, right here in your heart. Shine your light,
       baby girl. Sharing the love of Jesus is the perfect start.
       When you are here, HE will guide you."
Mrs. Key had tears in her eyes. She looked at her husband
and gave him a hug.

A little later, Shaun smiled at Peter and said,
"This is my stop. Thanks again. I can't wait
to meet everyone."
As soon as the bus stopped and the driver opened
the door, Shaun jumped down from the bus step
and ran into his house.

Seeing his mom in the kitchen, Shaun said,
"Mom, Mom, Jesus for the win! He used me;
yes, He did. I am an incredibly thankful kid.
HE is with me, right here in my heart. Sharing
the love of Jesus was and is the perfect start."

About Kharis Publishing:

Kharis Publishing, an imprint of Kharis Media LLC, is a leading Christian and inspirational book publisher based in Aurora, Chicago metropolitan area, Illinois. Kharis' dual mission is to give voice to under-represented writers (including women and first-time authors) and equip orphans in developing countries with literacy tools. That is why, for each book sold, the publisher channels some of the proceeds into providing books and computers for orphanages in developing countries so that these kids may learn to read, dream, and grow. For a limited time, Kharis Publishing is accepting unsolicited queries for nonfiction (Christian, self-help, memoirs, business, health and wellness) from qualified leaders, professionals, pastors, and ministers. Learn more at: **https://kharispublishing.com/**